THE OWL'S
L

NICK BUTTERWORTH

TED SMART

Swallows and swifts flew high above the head of Percy the park keeper. Soon they would be off on their long winter holidays. Some birds had already gone.

Percy was thinking how nice it would be to join them, but his thoughts were soon brought back down to earth.

"**P**ercy! Look what we've found!"
Just ahead of him, a squirrel friend
and the mole were standing over a heap
of twigs.

"Hello," said Percy. "That looks like an
old nest." He picked it up. "I shouldn't
think anyone lives in it now."

"Then you'd be wrong," said a little voice. A small feathery head stuck itself out from beneath the twigs. "I live in it. And you're holding me upside down."

"I'm so sorry," said Percy. He turned the nest over. "I thought you would have gone with your friends and relations."

"Can't fly," said the little bird. "I didn't get the hang of it."

"Oh dear," Percy began, but he wasn't allowed to finish.

"Good morning!"
It was the owl.

"Owl!" called Percy. "Can you help?
This little fellow can't fly."

"Flying?" said the owl, as she swooped
overhead. "Nothing to it," she hooted,
as she went into an impressive spin.
"Just flap and go!"

The owl shot up into the air and out
of sight. Almost at once, she was back
again, flying just above their heads.

"You see," she cooed,
    "it's easy. . ."
"Look out!" shouted Percy. . .

THUMP!
   The owl
hit a pine tree.
   Pine cones
rained down
on the squirrel
and the mole,

followed by the
owl in a dazed
and untidy heap.

"Well," said Percy, "I think there's a lesson for us all."

"Percy," said the squirrel, "have you got any string?" Percy felt in his pocket.

"Here's a piece," he said. "Why do you want it?"

The squirrel jumped to his feet.
"Come on," he said to the little
bird. "I'll give you a piggy-back."

Percy looked puzzled as the squirrel
began to climb a tree with a very
nervous passenger on his back.
"He needs to get used to heights,"
explained the squirrel.

W hen he reached the top, the squirrel tied the string between two branches.

"It's a tightrope," he said. "Follow me!"

alancing carefully, the squirrel stepped onto the string. The little bird bravely followed.

"Hooray!" cheered the mole.

"Well done!" called Percy. "We'll have you taking to the air in no time."

At that very moment, with a twang!
one of the squirrel's knots came
undone and the tightrope walkers found
themselves falling.

The squirrel managed to grab the end of the string. The little bird didn't. As he looked down, he expected to see the ground rushing towards him. Instead, he saw Percy, holding out his cap.

The little bird fell right into Percy's cap, but so hard, that he bounced straight out again.

"Oh no!" shouted Percy. "He's going to fall into those thorn bushes. Fly! Fly!"

And, as if he'd been doing it all his life, that's just what the little bird did. He flew. Away from the thorns, up into the air and perched at the top of the tree.

"Don't stop," called the owl.
"You can go after your friends
and relations now."

The little bird looked delighted.
"I will!" he called back.
"Thank you everybody!"
and with that he was off
over the tree tops.

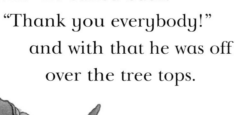

"Don't mention it," said a voice dangling from a piece of string halfway up a tree. "Don't mention it."

NICK BUTTERWORTH

Nick Butterworth was born in North
London in 1946 and grew up in a
sweet shop in Essex. He now lives
in Suffolk with his wife Annette
and their two children,
Ben and Amanda.

The inspiration for the Percy the Park Keeper books
came from Nick Butterworth's many walks through the
local park with the family dog, Jake. The stories have
now been made into a stunning animated television
series, available on video from HIT Entertainment plc.